A Cassava Republic Press edition 2017

First published in Belgium by De Eenhoorn
© Text and illustration: Mylo Freeman

Original Title: Prinses Arabella is jarig
Copyright 2006 by Uitgeverij De Eenhoorn, Vlasstraat 17, B-8710 Wielsbeke
(Belgium)

Translated from Dutch by Laura Watkinson

ISBN 978-1-911115-37-3

A CIP catalogue record for this book is available from the British Library.

The publisher gratefully acknowledges the support of the Dutch Foundation for
Literature and the Mondriaan Fund.

**N ederlands
letterenfonds
dutch foundation
for literature**

www.cassavarepublic.biz

MYLO FREEMAN

Princess Arabella's Birthday

CASSAVA REPUBLIC

Once upon a time, there was a little princess called Arabella. She lived in a big palace with her father, the King, and her mother, the Queen. It was nearly Arabella's birthday. But what do you give a little princess who already has everything?

"My dearest little Arabella," said the King.

"What would you like for your birthday?"

Princess Arabella thought long and hard.

"How about some roller skates with rubies on them?" asked the Queen.

"I already have a pair," answered Princess Arabella.

"A golden bike?"

"Got one," answered the princess.

SPECIAL

WOW!

"A cuddly mouse?"

"Got one," answered the princess.

AMAZING

"A rocking zebra?"

"Got one."

"A tea set? A doll's pram? A...?" "Got them all already!"
shouted Princess Arabella." No, I want something different."

FABULOUS!

"What I want is... an elephant!"

"An ELE-WHAT?!" gasped the Queen.

"Oh dear, oh dear," muttered the King. "Where are we going to find a creature like that? And who's going to take it for walks?"

Princess Arabella paid no attention. She wanted an elephant – and she was going to have one!

The next day, the King sent out his footmen to look for an elephant. They were away for seven days and seven nights.

And on the eighth day, they came back.

With an elephant.

Finally, it was the big day. Princess Arabella's birthday! She opened her eyes that morning and found her present waiting for her. Arabella was so happy that she clapped and danced around the elephant. "I'm going to play with her right away," she cried.

"Sit, Elephant! Sit!"

Elephant just stood there, gazing sadly into the distance.
"Hey, you're my present! You have to play with me!"
Arabella said. But Elephant didn't budge. Slowly, a big fat
tear trickled down her trunk. And another and
another. Princess Arabella was soon up to
her ankles in a puddle of tears.

"Stop that!" she ordered.

"Before I drown!"

"I want to go home!" sobbed Elephant. "Princess Arabella, take me back." "But... but that's not allowed," the princess protested. "You're my present!"

But when Elephant started trumpeting and wailing, she quickly said, "Elephant, please stop that crying this instant! I'll take you back right now!"

On the way to Elephant's home, Princess Arabella saw lots and lots of other amazing animals. "I want that one, and that one, and that one too!" she cried. Elephant hurried past...

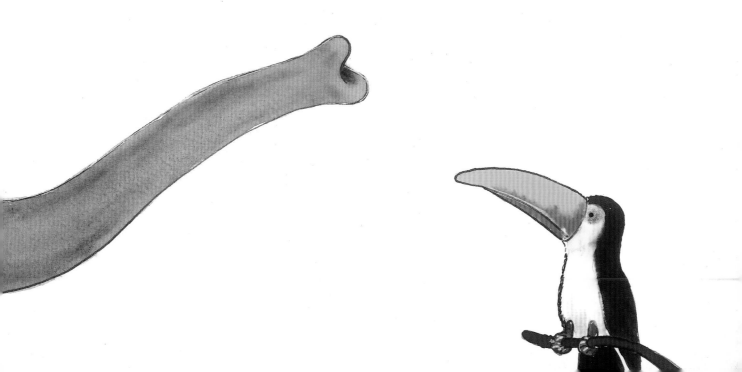

When they finally reached the place where Elephant lived, a baby elephant ran to meet them.

"Mama! You're home just in time and you've brought me my present!"

"Yes, little one," Elephant replied, "and it's exactly what you wanted...

... A real little princess!"